THIS CANDLEWICK BOOK BELONGS TO:

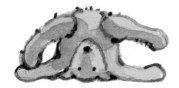

For Sue Seabrook C.T.

Text copyright © 1994 by Kathy Henderson
Illustrations copyright © 1994 by Carol Thompson

First U.S. paperback edition 1996

The Library of Congress has cataloged the hardcover edition as follows:

Henderson, Kathy, 1949–
Bounce, bounce, bounce / Kathy Henderson ; illustrated by Carol Thompson.—
1st U.S. ed.
Summary: In illustrations and rhyming text, an active toddler
demonstrates how water is meant for washing (splash splash splash),
chairs for sitting (bounce bounce bounce), and saucepans
for cooking (crash crash crash).
ISBN 1-56402-311-7 (hardcover)
[1. Play—Fiction.   2. Stories in rhyme.]   I. Thompson, Carol, ill.   II. Title.
PZ8.3.H4144Bo   1994
[E]—dc20   93-3556

ISBN 1-56402-669-8 (paperback)

2 4 6 8 10 9 7 5 3 1

Printed in Hong Kong

This book was typeset in M Baskerville.
The pictures were done in watercolor and ink.

Candlewick Press
2067 Massachusetts Avenue
Cambridge, Massachusetts 02140

Bounce Bounce Bounce

Kathy Henderson

illustrated by Carol Thompson

CANDLEWICK PRESS
CAMBRIDGE, MASSACHUSETTS

Chairs are for sitting on.

Bounce bounce bounce!

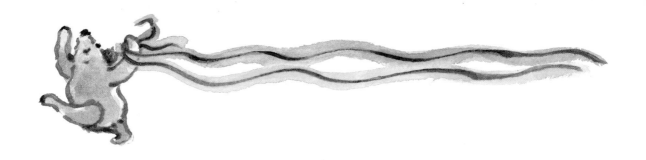

Beds are for
lying on.

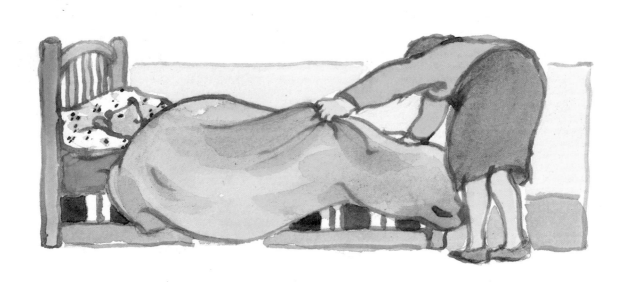

Dance dance dance!

Teddies are for
cuddling.

Up in the air and down!

And clothes are for
putting on.

Round and round and round!

Saucepans are for
cooking in.

Crash crash crash!

Water is for
washing with.

Splash splash splash!

Cribs are for
sleeping in.

Squeak squeak squeak!

And parents,
what are parents for?

Sleep sleep sleep!

KATHY HENDERSON worked in publishing for a number of years before turning to writing and illustrating children's books. Her books for children include *Bumpety Bump,* also illustrated by Carol Thompson; *The Little Boat,* illustrated by Patrick Benson; and *Sam and the Big Machines,* named one of *Parents Magazine*'s "Best Books for Babies." With *Bounce Bounce Bounce* she wanted to "capture children's glorious, gleeful capacity to explore. To them, beds aren't just for lying on."

CAROL THOMPSON is an award-winning fabric designer, as well as an illustrator of children's books, including Joyce Dunbar's *Oops-a-Daisy!* She recalls, "When I first saw this text, I was delighted with how lovely it was to read. As I began to illustrate it, I realized that its simplicity was deceptive. I worked with the author very closely in order to make my pictures as seemingly simple and effortless as the words."